Felicity

Felicity

Susan Budd

Escape Books
New York

Publisher's Cataloging-in-Publication Data

Budd, Susan, 1963-
Felicity / Susan Budd.
pages cm
ISBN 978-0-9907773-1-1 (pbk.)
1. Fantasy fiction.   I. Title.
PS3602.U333F45 2015
813'.6—dc23

I.

She knew she had been captured. She didn't know how or why. She didn't know who they were. She didn't even know who she was. But she knew she had been captured and brought here.

She had no memory of anything before this moment. A strange fact, but she didn't notice. She was only dimly aware of her surroundings. Her mind was fully conscious, but her awareness was fragmentary and only gradually did she notice her captors. They were five.

"You're ours now. You understand that, right? You're ours." The voice was pleasant, conciliatory.

She was sitting and the man who spoke stood in front of her. A woman sat at her side smiling at her joyfully. Nearby were three others. Two men, who stood on either side of her as if to prevent her escape. And a woman who swayed lightly from side to side as if she could barely keep from dancing in delight.

They seemed to be talking about her, but she couldn't make out their words. They seemed far away. The part of her mind that wanted to ask a hundred questions seemed to be asleep.

She looked around. She couldn't see very far. It was as if the air were thick. What she could see were sofas like the one on which she sat. She saw pillows and cushions on the plush carpeting. And all in pale shades of ivory, gray, and beige. It was soft and luxurious.

The woman who was light on her feet handed her a steaming cup of clear colorless liquid. She took it and inhaled the steam. It was jasmine. She looked at the liquid. It was golden. She sipped her tea.

"I'm Fae," the woman said. Fae had a kind face. She took back the empty tea cup and received a smile of thanks.

"See, she likes us," Fae said to the others. "What should we call her?" And without waiting for a response, "Mimi. Let's call her Mimi." Fae alone was full of energy. Everyone else was still a little out of breath. And Mimi was exhausted. She just hadn't noticed before.

She heard them talking about her again and this time she could make out some of what they were saying. "She needs to sleep," one of the men said. He had explained it to Fae before, to all of them before. They didn't really understand. Naturally. It was a meaningless concept. But they accepted it.

"Come see your room." Fae sounded excited. Mimi followed her a few paces to the opposite wall and Fae slid open a door. The others maintained their positions beside and behind her, as if she might yet try to flee.

The room was small and windowless, but refreshingly cool. Only when the cool air touched Mimi's skin did she become aware of how over-heated she had been. A mattress was on the floor. She lay down upon it. It was soft and luxurious.

She didn't even see them leave.

II.

Her kimono sleeve was half covering her face. She woke up with the cool silk brushing her cheek. Mimi felt like she slept a long time, but she couldn't be sure. There was no clock. There were no windows. She didn't know if it was day or night. Though she felt like she slept a long time. There was light in the room, a subdued light that bespoke the dawn, but there was no source of illumination.

The bed covering upon which she lay was pumpkin-colored cotton with a paisley print that felt familiar. It hadn't been there when she went to sleep. Or had it, and she just too tired to notice? She didn't recall ever seeing it before, but it felt comfortably familiar. So did the kimono. It was blue batik, the blue subtly graduating from azure to violet, the design intricate and delicate. Was it hers? She hadn't been wearing it when she went to sleep. Or had she? She didn't recall what she had been wearing when she went to sleep.

Mimi wasn't troubled by these mysteries, just mildly curious. She picked up a hot cup of tea that sat on a low table by her bedside. She didn't even wonder how it came to be there, or how it could still be hot if it had been placed there before she awoke. Instead she nestled into the pillows, blowing on the surface of her tea and drinking it in small sips.

The room was small but it didn't feel confining. Quite the opposite. It felt peaceful, tranquil. And the pale and neutral color scheme, so soft and sleepy, was livened up by the paisley bed covering and her bright blue kimono.

Only one thing troubled Mimi, and it didn't trouble her all that much. The room had no door. It didn't seem possible for a room to have no door. She had come in through the door. Of that she was certain. Yet there was no door.

She looked in her cup to see if any tea remained. It was full. And piping hot. And she was glad of it. As she sipped, she noticed lights reflected on the surface of her tea. The reflections came from the multicolored fairy lights strung on the walls. They were charming and Mimi was pleased to notice them. She also noticed that the wall that had no door did indeed have a door. It was a shōji door. The colored lights reflected off the translucent paper panels.

She still didn't know if it was day or night. It felt like morning because she had just woken up, because she felt refreshed. But she didn't know. She went to the door, put her hand lightly on the bamboo frame, and slid it open.

III.

"We did it. I can hardly believe it. We have a Felicity." Sunny spoke for all of them. Her voice was like the first flower of spring.

The capture of a Felicity was a rare event. And a gravely dangerous one. More people had been killed trying to capture one of the elusive creatures than ever benefited from having one. The household had been exceptionally fortunate. Not only did they succeed in capturing the Felicity, but not one life was lost.

Ryder advised caution. He was just as happy as the others, but his was the voice of reason. Although the situation looked promising, they had to be careful. They didn't risk their lives to capture the Felicity only to let her get away. Yet they also didn't want to alarm her by appearing to be sitting guard at her door.

It was finally decided that Fae and Tripp would be the first ones she would see when she emerged from her room. They had already spoken to her, and all had gone well, so she might feel more at ease with just the two of them. Ryder would remain out of sight on one side of the door and Sunny and Wave on the other. If need be, and Fae was certain there would be no need, the three could quickly step in.

The hours of waiting for Mimi to awaken did them all good. Their perilous adventure and the thrill of the capture had them all wound up. What they needed most if they wanted to appear casual around Mimi was to relax and occupy themselves with their usual activities.

Sunny devoted herself to her painting. It had been nearly finished when she had to rush out with the others to capture the Felicity before anyone else did. It amused her to recall how displeased she had been to have to stop when it was nearly finished, and now, now the Felicity was truly theirs. Wave watched her paint and strummed dreamily on his guitar.

Ryder returned to the mathematical con-undrum he had been exploring. At first he was over-excited and couldn't concentrate, but after a little while his mind settled down and he got back to what Fae liked to call his "equations and particles."

Tripp was reciting his latest poem to Fae when Mimi came out of her room.

Dogwood trees in bloom,
Walking through the avenues—
Snow flowers in spring.

She joined them on their sofa and Fae insisted that Tripp recite his poem again for Mimi's amusement. When he finished Fae clapped and so did Mimi.

IV.

The sofas were sectional and arranged in little clusters on only one wall, the wall that was opposite Mimi's room. Mimi looked at the place where her shōji door should have been. It wasn't there, but its absence was less interesting to her than the curvature of the walls. The north and south walls curved so gradually into the distance that she couldn't even see the east and west walls. She thought to ask Fae about it, but didn't. A strange and powerful urge to be silent stopped her.

Perhaps Tripp saw her trying to peer around the curvature of the walls because he suggested a tour of the house.

As the three walked the curve remained the same and Mimi saw more of the sectional sofas. Each cluster was arranged in a different configuration. Had they not been differently arranged Mimi might have believed she was looking at the same scene over and over again, for as much as they walked they never came to a wall. How long had they been walking?

She became aware of a faint sound, the rhythmic strumming of a guitar. The sound grew clearer and then Wave came into view. And after him Sunny.

Sunny was painting on the wall opposite the sofas. She painted as if from some inner need. The bright bold colors seemed brighter and bolder in comparison with the neutral shades everywhere else. Everywhere else except Mimi, that is, in her bright blue kimono.

Mimi watched her paint. She had the feeling that something was unusual about Sunny's painting, but she didn't know what. Sunny painted thick swirls of yellow. The yellow swirls coursed between shapeless masses of orange and red. A single desultory line of rich purple wound its way through the whole of it.

Sunny glided from one side of her painting to the other on nimble feet. Her white dress swished around her knees as she moved. Her arms made graceful circles through the air as her sensitive hands created the brilliant swirls.

That was it. That was what was so unusual. She had no paintbrush. She had no paint. It was her hands that made the painting, her hands that applied the color.

"Let's take you to see Ryder next," Tripp said after a while. But instead of going forward, he turned in the direction from which they had come. Mimi was puzzled. With a quizzical look, she pointed in the direction she was expecting them to take.

Wave laughed. "She doesn't understand." Then he looked at Mimi and explained. "It's a circle, a ring." He traced a circle in the air with his finger. "You go all the way around and end up right where you started."

"How cute," Fae chirped.

Tripp smiled indulgently. "Then on with the tour." He turned around and led the way.

Even though she knew she was walking in a circle, it didn't feel like it. The clusters of furniture were the same. Nothing distinguished itself from the rest of the house. But this time the walk seemed much shorter.

Ryder soon came into view. He was reclining on a sofa, waiting for them. They joined him and Mimi was glad to sit down. The air was too warm for her and it made her feel weak.

"You should eat," Ryder said to her. He handed her a bowl of small colorless wafers. It didn't interest her. She wasn't hungry. She should have been hungry. She couldn't remember the last time she ate. But she wasn't in the least hungry.

Ryder held his own bowl and so did Tripp and Fae. Mimi hadn't noticed the bowls before. Had they been out of sight until now? Ryder took a square cracker from his bowl and ate it conspicuously. Fae and Tripp also ate from their bowls. Yellow triangular chips for Tripp. And a pink custard for Fae that she ate daintily with a spoon.

Mimi reached into her bowl. It held, not colorless wafers, but ginger snaps. She bit into one. The sweet and spicy flavor was familiar and pleasant. After she finished her cookie she set her bowl down, but Ryder urged her to eat more.

"Our food is not very nutritious," he explained. "So you have to eat more of it." Mimi took up her bowl and bit into another ginger snap. They all looked pleased at her ready acquiescence.

V.

There was no way to tell how much Mimi understood. According to lore, a Felicity was a simple-minded being. But little was known with certainty.

No one knew where they came from. No one really knew what they were. Or why they were. That the Felicity was rare was a given. In fact, there were those who didn't even believe the creatures existed. Now or ever. Not one had been discovered in centuries. The last Felicity anyone had heard of lived nearly a thousand years ago. And even that was not beyond doubt.

They may have existed in abundance in times past. Or they may have always been as rare as they were now. Being entirely anecdotal, the lore was often inconsistent. Some people believed that periods of abundance alternated with periods of scarcity, while others said that it was random.

However, there were a few things that were generally held. A Felicity was female and looked much like an ordinary woman except that she tended to be more petite. She lived at most seventy or eighty years, not counting the years prior to capture. Moreover, she spent about a third of her short life in a state called "sleep."

A sleeping Felicity may appear to be simply lying down with her eyes closed, but there's much more to sleep than that. In sleep, a Felicity is unaware of anything going on around her. Nor is she thinking about anything. She is as unaware of herself as she is of her surroundings. A loud noise or a nudge will bring her out of this state, usually with a start. But if left undisturbed she will come out of it naturally after a while.

Sleep is apparently essential for the Felicity. She will usually know when she is about to enter the state and will seek privacy. A room should be provided for her. This room should be kept cool. The Felicity prefers a cooler temperature and will retreat to this room when she feels overheated.

The mysterious creatures did have the capacity for speech. Though by all accounts they seldom made use of it. It was commonly believed that this reticence was due to their low intelligence. However it was also possible that their characteristic silence was unrelated to their intellectual shortcomings. The only thing that was agreed upon was that they were disinclined to speak. So far, Mimi was no exception.

And then there was the one truly undeniable fact. Nothing was more deadly than a captive Felicity. Not even the tigers who prowled the outer region. A Felicity who wanted to escape would destroy anyone in her path.

There was no way to tell how much Mimi understood, but she appeared to be content in her new home. And that was fortunate. Very fortunate.

VI.

Something was about to begin. Mimi was waiting for it. They all were. What were they waiting for? Mimi didn't know. Though she knew they were all waiting eagerly.

Sunny and Tripp lounged side by side on a sofa, their fingers interlaced. Mimi sat across from them and Ryder sat on a floor cushion. Fae and Wave conferred excitedly out of earshot.

Then it began. The music rose gradually. It seemed to come from nowhere. It was Wave's composition. Finally completed.

The drumbeat rose, a backbeat rhythm. Fae came forward, bathed in a rainbow of light. The bass, thick and heavy, shaped her movements.

Wave stood smiling, listening to his rhythm, basking in it, tapping his foot and bobbing his head in time.

But all eyes were on Fae. As she twirled and danced, the long full skirt of her white dress billowed around her. The points of its handkerchief hem rose and fell, now skimming her ankles, now fluttering gracefully.

On she danced, bejeweled in the colored lights. And the rhythm grew. Mimi felt it, felt the rhythm, first in her feet and then in her hips. She was dancing too. They all were.

Fae moved her arms, directing multicolored beams of light over all the dancers. The colors made dazzling patterns on Sunny's white dress, on the white kurtas and trousers of the men, on the white and gray and beige furniture.

Then haze arose. It rippled around their feet, softening the colors, melting them, blending them into ever more subtle shades.

Mimi danced in the opal glow that ebbed and flowed with the rhythm. She danced blissfully. She danced for days. Or so it seemed. She didn't know. She didn't care. She was happy.

VII.

Mimi was fascinated. It wasn't the poem Tripp was reading aloud that fascinated her. It was the book from which he read. As Mimi and Sunny sat eating from their bowls, Tripp regaled them with the poems he had heard the last time he went to the Fair.

He held the book in two hands. It was a large clothbound book. Entirely white. Mimi noticed that there was nothing printed anywhere on the exterior of the book. She noticed because she deliberately looked. She expected something to be there and was puzzled to see nothing.

Tripp held the book open in the middle and never turned the page. He had read a good many poems too. He should have had to turn the page, yet not once did he do so. Mimi was certain, for she was watching.

Sunny sometimes asked questions, but her questions were always about the poets, not the poems. She liked to know who they were and where they came from, how they looked and what they did. Tripp told all he had seen and heard.

All the while Mimi inched closer to Tripp. Boldly and bashfully. She wanted to peer into the book. And when she did see within the book, she saw a single poem, just three short lines on the clean white paper. Tripp read the poem aloud and Mimi's eyes followed the words on the page.

"Do you like it?" he asked, perceiving her curiosity. She glanced at him and nodded. "Then I'll read you another."

Mimi returned her eyes to the book. A different poem was on the page. Tripp read. This time Mimi kept her eyes on the page.

Sunny wanted to know who it was who created such a pleasant poem and Tripp described the poet to her. Still Mimi kept her eyes on the page.

Then Tripp began to read the next poem. And indeed, a new poem was now on the page. Yet Mimi had not looked away, not for a moment. She was so bemused that she nearly asked Tripp to explain.

Perhaps he did divine that her interest lay in the book itself and not the poems, for he closed the book and offered it to her. "You can have it if you like."

Mimi liked. She turned the book over in her hands, looking at the front, the back, the spine. She opened it and flipped through the pages with her thumb. Not a word. It was blank. She looked at Tripp, then at Sunny.

Sunny pointed to the book. "How charming."

Mimi held a slender paperback in her hand. How charming indeed. She was delighted. She flipped through the book. It was filled. She showed it to Sunny and Tripp.

Sunny marveled at the illustration on the cover. Especially the colors, the yellow, green, and purple. She found the drawing whimsical, the little boy, his tiny world, the sun and stars. But it was the colors that most appealed to her. She found it peculiar that a poem was inscribed on the drawing.

But she liked its green and purple words. She was less pleased with the illustrations within, for they were not in color.

Tripp read the book's cover aloud, to hear the sound of it. "What is a prince?" he asked. Mimi pointed to the little boy in the illustration. Tripp opened the book in the middle and gazed at two full pages of type. Then he flipped though the pages as Mimi had done. "What a long poem it is." He handed it back to Mimi.

VIII.

Mimi had learned a few things in the days, or was it months, since she had come to be here. She learned to eat continuously. She learned to retreat to her room when she became overheated. And she learned to open the door to her room wherever she happened to be.

Although she was neither sleepy nor overheated, she wanted to read her book right away, so she slid the door to her room open.

She gathered the folds of her kimono around her and curled up on her bed. The multicolored fairy lights were aglow. Her food bowl and cup of tea sat on her little table. And the cool air was fresh and sweet. The soft illumination of the room was not fit for reading, but that caused her no trouble. The light was much brighter on her book.

She gazed at the cover. Sunny was right. It was a charming illustration. And the title, though not a poem, sounded as nice as a poem. *The Little Prince*. She opened the book at the beginning and started to read. The story seemed vaguely familiar, though she had never read it before. She had never read anything before.

Page after page she turned and as she did the story grew. It sprouted and ripened as she read. She did not know how long it took her to read it. But she read all the way through. And when it finally came to an end she relished it.

Mimi was drowsy, but she wanted to savor her story a little longer so she sat up and thought about all that she had just read. As she thought, the light became dimmer. She was almost asleep. Then she heard music. "Ripple." She didn't know if she actually heard it or just imagined she heard it. Not that it mattered. She slipped down to her pillow and wrapped her arms around it. The music played. And Mimi went to sleep.

IX.

"Wake up. Mimi. Wake up." Fae was terrified. She awoke Mimi from a sound sleep.

Outside of Mimi's room all was chaos. There was a heavy pounding sound that seemed to come from everywhere all at once. And a metallic scraping, high-pitched and grating, that came and went.

The ambient light was so low that Mimi and Fae could barely see the others, though they caught glimpses of movement as random flashes of white light broke the darkness for a second at a time.

The others rushed frantically here and there, moving around the outer wall, feeling it with their hands. Had it not been for the din, Mimi and Fae might have heard Sunny sobbing as she passed her hands over her section of the wall.

"They're in," Ryder shouted.

The pounding stopped. The metallic scraping stopped. And a bright light shone through a doorway that had not been there before. Men and women came through the doorway. They held clubs and knives. They meant harm. Harm to Mimi's household.

What happened next was never clearly recollected by anyone. Mimi changed.

As the men and women charged through the doorway, Mimi expanded into something amorphous, something vast and enormous. She loomed over the intruders, black as night and dazzling as the sun. It was difficult to look directly at her.

Then came the roar. The terrible awful roar. It sounded like the end of everything. It sounded like nothing anyone had ever heard before.

The nebulous something that was Mimi had no shape, no substance. Yet there were teeth. Too many teeth, razor-sharp and pointed. Mimi was angry. Her household was in danger and she was angry.

The intruders panicked. They didn't know where to run. There were six of them. Two made it to the doorway and didn't look back. The rest were caught, one by one. Lifted high up into the air and plunged into nothingness. It was a horror to behold.

Mimi ate them all up. And when it was over it was as if it had never happened. The doorway was gone. The light was back. Everything was as it had been. Except that Mimi lay on the white carpet, dazed and weak.

"She needs to rest." Ryder spoke calmly, authoritatively. Everyone else was in shock. He bent down beside Mimi and the others followed. She was barely conscious.

Together they put her to bed.

X.

There was no one in the world who wouldn't risk death in pursuit of a Felicity. Even with little chance of success. Two men and two women were lost in the failed invasion of Mimi's household. Yet there was not anyone in the world who wouldn't have done what they did.

What little hope they had of capturing Mimi lay in the possibility that she would not protect her household. Had she not been content in her new home, they might have slaughtered everyone and taken her for themselves. And even if she was content, as she was, they could still hope to kill everyone before she knew what was happening and then coax her into being theirs. The chance was remote, but a chance was a chance. They risked everything on it and they paid with four lives.

How many before them died such deaths? There was no way to know. There was nothing in the lore. Theoretically it would depend on how many of the beings had been discovered. But who can know that? If a household discovered a Felicity and perished trying to capture her, no one would know. It would also depend on whether more than one household made the discovery. If it was more than one, violence was inevitable. There was no one who wouldn't kill for a Felicity.

There was little suffering in the world. But there was still suffering.

There was no hunger, no poverty, no money, no caste. No one lacked for anything. No one was subject to anyone else. They all had everything they wanted. And because they all had everything they wanted, there was no greed, no envy, no theft, no quarreling.

The elimination of want, the technological provision of limitless material goods, made for a world of simplicity, peace, and comfort. But social evils were one thing and natural evils quite another.

Most of the maladies that had plagued their ancient ancestors had been eradicated. Most, but not all. There were still some illnesses. Fatal, incurable illnesses. There were still men and women who died young. There were still children who died. It didn't happen often, but when it happened it was terrible. It was something to dread. It could happen to anyone. Anyone at all. Except someone who had a Felicity.

There was no illness in a household with a Felicity. No one knew why this was so. But that it was so was certain. Having a Felicity was an assurance of life. And life was precious.

XI.

Mimi awoke in her bed. She didn't know how long she had slept. She never did. But this time there was something different about it. Waking up had always felt natural. She always woke up feeling refreshed. But not this time.

This time she awoke from a dream. A strange dream. Or at least it seemed like a dream. She couldn't be sure. Maybe it was a memory. A memory of something that happened long ago. A distant memory.

She remembered being woken up by Fae. She remembered the horrible noise, the darkness, the flashing light that hurt her eyes. She remembered the intruders. And what she had done to them.

But when did it all happen?

She felt as if her sleep had been troubled. As if she had swallowed something noxious. As if her body had been bloated and her mind uneasy.

How long had she slept? There was no way to know. She was never hungry or thirsty. Her hair and nails never grew. And she was always clean as the morning dew. So she never knew how long she had slept.

Everyday Sunny would paint. Tripp would compose poetry. Wave would make music. But their creations were ephemeral. Created one day and gone the next. There was never any sign of the passage of time.

She could have slept for a year. For all she knew, she could have slept for two.

XII.

It was nice to watch Sunny paint. Especially nice was that first stroke of color on the white wall. This time it was red. A bold red that spiraled upward.

Mimi reclined on a sofa. She heard Wave's voice. Then Tripp's. A moment later she saw them. They appeared around the curvature of the walls.

"It doesn't look like Sunny's coming," observed Tripp. "But you'll come, won't you Mimi?"

Wave put his hand on an area of the wall that Sunny hadn't gotten to yet. A doorway opened. Mimi was curious. She nodded.

The doorway led to an inner courtyard. Mimi was delighted. She had never been in the open air before. This was her first time. Though that seemed unlikely. Surely she had been somewhere before she came to be here. But this was the first time that she knew of, so she was delighted.

The stone tiles under her feet were cool and hard. A novelty in contrast to the plush carpeting inside. There were rattan sofas and lounges. Each with white cushions. The cushions were as soft and luxurious as the ones inside. Wave stretched himself out on a lounge chair. Tripp sat on a sofa. Mimi sat down too.

She looked up. There was no moon, no stars. Just a pearly gray sky with a streak of the palest pink. Neither growing nor fading. Twilight.

Was it dusk or dawn? Mimi couldn't tell. But it was beautiful.

Wave broke the silence. He wanted to hear Tripp's latest poem and Tripp was happy to recite it to his little audience.

> *Butterfly of gold*
> *Striped in bands of brilliant hue—*
> *A fragile tiger.*

Wave was meditative. His closed his eyes. Slowly he repeated Tripp's poem aloud. Then he smiled a broad smile and lifted a shakuhachi to his lips. The sound was ethereal.

His melody was simple. It evoked stillness. Stillness and peace. It was a twilight melody. In harmony with the surrounding silence. Mimi and Tripp listened. The lilt of the bamboo flute was like the rustle of leaves in a breeze. Transcendent and pure. The breathy sound of the instrument mingled with the scent of wisteria in the air.

Mimi inhaled deeply the rich floral aroma. It had not been there before. She felt sure of it. She would have noticed. It was too lovely not to notice.

She would have liked to see the flowers, but she couldn't see very far in the twilight so she got up and took a few steps onto the grass. The grass was lush and tickled her feet pleasantly. She walked towards the center of the courtyard. She meant to walk to the opposite side, though she had no way of knowing how far that might be. If she knew the size of the house she could have known the size of the courtyard, but she didn't know the size of the house. She didn't even know if she had ever made a full circuit of the house.

She walked a long time without reaching the other side. It felt good to walk on the grass, smelling the wisteria and hearing the delicate sound of the shakuhachi. No matter how long she walked the sound of Wave's flute never got any fainter. It was as if she had not walked any distance at all.

When she decided to return to her sofa, it was only a few steps away.

The pink streak of light in the gray sky was just as it was when she first saw it. Neither more nor less. It made Mimi wonder. If she waited, would night fall or would the sun rise? Would the stars appear or would a new day dawn?

She would have liked to find out, but she fell asleep before anything happened.

XIII.

The three of them were laughing. A merry laughter. Mimi liked it. They were sitting on floor cushions, Fae, Sunny, and Wave, and they were tossing a soft fabric ball back and forth.

They invited Mimi to play. She sat on a floor cushion and the game resumed. Fae was holding the ball. Her eyes were half closed and she rocked gently in place. She looked euphoric. Then she tossed the ball to Wave and her trance immediately dissipated. Meanwhile his face took on a faraway look.

Mimi's turn was next. She cupped her hands and Wave tossed the ball to her. The moment it touched her hands her perceptions were distorted. Shapes became shapeless. Contours dissolved. Everything wavered and shimmered, silvery and vibrant. Everything pulsed with life. Colors morphed before her eyes, as if she were looking through a kaleidoscope. It was beautiful and fantastic and sublime.

Mimi felt the space around her body, felt it as a palpable presence caressing every inch of her flesh. Was she still sitting on a floor cushion? Or was she afloat on supple liquid air? Or drifting through a sea of foam?

Eons of serenity passed before Mimi remembered the soft fabric ball in her hands. She tossed it to Sunny.

XIV.

Ryder knew more lore than anyone and he had never heard of a Felicity reading. The thought disturbed him, though he didn't know why.

When Tripp told him about Mimi and her book with the colorful illustration of a little boy, he didn't think much about it. Not at first. But then, he hadn't given much thought to Mimi since her capture. He had been much too busy.

Ryder took little interest in the arts and enjoyments of the others. He aspired to stewardship, an honor only bestowed upon the most learned of physicists and mathematicians. So he was always studying. But the more he thought about Mimi reading, the more it disturbed him.

It probably meant nothing. He didn't even know if she was actually reading. She might just be looking at the pictures. And even if she could read, what did it matter if she amused herself with poetry? It was an innocent enough pastime. Though unusual, it probably meant nothing. Just that Mimi was brighter than the average Felicity.

To put his mind at ease, he decided to investigate.

He tapped on Mimi's door. She was reading and Ryder asked to see what it was. He sat on the floor. She handed the book to him. A slender cloth-bound book. He read the title out loud. *Meditations on First Philosophy*. He opened it and began to read.

What he read disturbed him greatly. It wasn't a pretty little poem. It was metaphysical speculation. An inquiry into the nature of existence. First philosophy. The ultimate questions. How could Mimi be reading this? It shouldn't be possible.

Ryder didn't know what to make of it, but he knew he should put a stop to it. Metaphysics was no plaything for a Felicity.

"You shouldn't have this Mimi," he said as gently as he could.

He got up to leave with the book. He didn't like having to take it away from her. She looked unhappy. In sympathy he added, "One of the others can give you a more suitable toy." And he left.

Tripp, Wave, and Fae were sitting on the sofas when Ryder left Mimi's room. They were talking. Sunny was painting.

Then Mimi came out of her room. She glared at Ryder. Everyone sensed that something was amiss. Everyone except Sunny, who had not looked away from her painting, but soon would.

Mimi roared. She glared at Ryder and roared. That same terrible awful roar they had heard once before. Sunny whirled around to see what the others were seeing.

The outline of Mimi wavered. Darkened and wavered. But only for an instant. Then she fled into her room.

XV.

Mimi felt sad. She didn't like feeling sad. Not one bit. But the sadness was upon her and all she could do was to bear it the best she could.

She didn't want to eat or drink. She didn't want to hear her music or look at her multicolored fairy lights. She wanted her book back. But more than that, she wanted Ryder to not have taken it from her.

She wrapped her kimono tightly around herself and curled up on her bed. She looked at the wall where there was sometimes a shōji door. There was no door there now. Maybe there would never be a door there again. Why should there be? She rolled over, turning her back to the wall where the door sometimes was.

She laid like that a long time. Or what seemed like a long time. She had gone numb. Then a tap on the door roused her. It was Ryder. She sat up and looked at him.

"This is yours." He held out her book to her. "I'm sorry."

He was humble and his humility moved Mimi. She took her book and gave him a smile of simple gratitude, with no trace of resentment.

"May I?" he asked, indicating with a wave of his hand the place on the floor where he had sat on his previous visit. She nodded. He sat and hesitated. "I wondered what you thought of it."

Mimi hesitated as well. She felt bashful. She looked at the book in her lap. Then she looked back up and answered him.

"Descartes seeks mathematical certainty." Mimi paused. She never heard her own voice before. It was soft and deliberate. She continued. "He proves his existence through reason because he trusts only logic and geometry. He distrusts the senses because they are fallible, because they can be doubted. But he does not doubt that he thinks, that he is a thinking thing."

"He *cannot* doubt that he thinks," said Ryder. "The products of reason alone are certain."

Mimi responded slowly. She was not yet accustomed to her voice. "He exists whether he thinks or not. He relies too much on reason."

"Only through reason can anything be known." Ryder spoke with conviction. "What the senses perceive could be false. His experience of the world could be a dream."

"And what if it is a dream?" Mimi replied. "Reason is not enough. Where is wisdom?"

Ryder pondered Mimi's words. "I'm glad you're here Mimi. I'm glad you're here with us." Mimi was glad too.

Ryder fell silent. He looked at Mimi differently. And Mimi felt it. She didn't know what it was, but she felt it. Ryder moved closer to her. He sat on the mattress beside her. Then he pressed his lips to hers.

She should have been astonished. She knew nothing of passion. She knew nothing of kisses. She had never even seen a kiss. But she was too pleased to register surprise. She wanted it to continue.

Ryder was clumsy at first. It was his first kiss too. But the two of them soon found their groove. They enfolded each other in their arms and their passion intensified.

Then Mimi started to understand what was happening. He wanted to mate with her. And she wanted it too, but somehow she knew she should not. Though desire urged her on, instinct compelled her to stop.

Mimi didn't know what she was, but whatever she was, she wasn't one of them. "We mustn't," she said in a barely audible voice.

Ryder understood immediately. It was as if he had some intuition of his own. "I know," he whispered.

He stood up and gazed at her with affection. "I'm glad you're here Mimi." She smiled in reply. Then he slid open the door.

XVI.

Mimi had an idea. She walked up to the wall. Not the wall where there was sometimes a door, but the wall on the other side of her room. She raised her hand just as she would to slid a door open and a door that had not been there before slid open. She stepped into the courtyard.

It seemed smaller than when she had walked in the twilight. But it was bright. The sky was blue and everything was bathed in sunshine. Glorious sunshine.

Mimi looked down while her eyes adjusted. Under her feet the stone tiles were warm. The air was fresh and clean. She inhaled deeply. There was no scent of wisteria. There was no scent of anything. Not yet.

In the center of the courtyard was a circular plot of earth. It was surrounded by a ring of grass which in turn was surrounded by the tiled patio with its rattan furniture. The furniture was spaced at regular intervals just as it was inside the house.

Mimi walked across the grass to the waiting plot of earth. A light breeze barely ruffled her hair. She stepped onto the soil. It felt soft and moist between her toes. She was ready to begin.

She got down on her knees. Down on her knees in the fertile black earth. Then she started turning the soil with a hand rake.

Beside her was a basket. It held little packets of seeds. After she had loosened the soil, she took a garden trowel and dug a hole. She placed a seed inside and smoothed the soil over it. Then she dug another hole. And another. This she did until she had a row of freshly planted seeds. When she finished, she started on the next row.

Mimi didn't know how long she worked in her garden. There were a lot of seeds to sow, but she never wearied. She liked the way the soil felt in her hands and it gave her satisfaction to pat it down over each little seed. After she planted the last seed in the last row she stood up and looked over her work. It was good. She was pleased with it.

She brushed the soil off the bottom of her kimono and went back inside.

XVII.

Sitting still did not come easily to Fae. While Sunny sat blithely eating tiny round cakes from her bowl, Fae just swirled her spoon in her custard without eating.

"Do you think she'll wake up soon?" she asked.

Sunny shrugged her shoulders.

Fae set her bowl down and stood up. She twirled on her heels a few times and then rearranged the sofa pillows. "What do you think she does out there?"

Sunny shrugged her shoulders again. "I don't know," she said between bites. She was curious, but not quite as curious as Fae.

By the time Mimi came out of her room, Fae had become so eager to pose her question that she couldn't even wait for Mimi to sit down on the sofa.

Mimi was not at all troubled by Fae's impatience. She immediately went to the inner wall and opened a door to the courtyard. Fae and Sunny followed. What they saw when they passed through the doorway was dazzling. The bright blue sky. The sunshine. The clouds agleam with light. And in the center of it all, the garden, green with life.

Mimi tended to a tomato plant that needed pruning. Fae watched her work. Sunny gazed at the sky.

The plants were strong and healthy, for Mimi tended them well.

As Fae bent over a tomato plant to take a closer look, she smelled the pungent aroma of the foliage. It was a sharp smell, crisp and peppery. She walked carefully between the rows of sprouting vegetables. The tomato plants already had small green fruit. So did the pepper plants. The lettuce and spinach plants were full of leaves. And the tops of radishes and carrots rose out of the soil. Fae ran the fine fronds of a carrot lightly through her fingers.

Sunny was still gazing at the sky when Fae called her over to see the plants. Sunny looked closely at the leaves and stems and unripe fruit. Each with its own shade of green.

As Sunny and Fae admired the garden, the first drop fell. It landed on a spinach leaf and glittered in the sunshine. Fae didn't see it, but Sunny did. She saw it and she sighed, awed by the beauty of it. She crouched beside the spinach, rapt in contemplation of the glittering raindrop. And more drops fell. They fell lightly at first, splashing on the soil, the plants, the patio tiles.

When the scattered drops became a shower, Sunny, Fae, and Mimi took cover under an awning that Mimi had never noticed before. Still the sun shone in the bright blue sky.

They stood only a moment under the awning. Then Fae cast a playful glance at Mimi and Sunny before dashing into the sun shower. Mimi and Sunny were right behind her, dancing and laughing in the rain. The picture of grace.

They danced in a circle around the garden, water dripping from their hair, from their clothes. They tossed their heads back and raised their arms to the sky and the rain streamed down their faces.

And around they danced. Round and round on the wet grass. In the shimmering sunshine. In the rain. The rain that watered Mimi's garden.

XVIII.

Sunny stood before the white wall but did not see it. Instead she saw her next painting, as vivid in her mind as if it were already completed. It was a joyful vision. She was ready to begin. She lingered only to relish the inspiration. The irresistible urge to transform feeling into color.

She was aware of Mimi sitting behind her on a sofa. She could sense Mimi's presence. She always could. It didn't matter if she could see her. Mimi's nearness was enough to fill Sunny with bliss. None of the others seemed to be affected in this way.

Tripp thought Mimi was smart because she was responsive to poetry and because she could read. Wave thought Tripp was just seeing what he wanted to see. They each had an idea about how much Mimi knew. But it did not matter to Sunny what Mimi knew. What mattered to Sunny was what Mimi was. She was a Felicity. A mysterious being, transcendental and sublime.

What truths lay within her? What depths? What profundities beyond the scope of the intellect? Sunny didn't know. But she knew that Mimi was the source of her bliss.

Sunny lifted her hand as high as she could and swept it across the white wall. Where her hand had been the wall was as blue as the blue in her mind. A beautiful blue like the sky. Vast and cool and clear. It expanded under her touch. It spread across the wall.

Sunny's movements were swift and natural. She gave form to her vision as never before. She reached down towards the floor and drew her hand upward with a flourish, leaving a trail of green. Then again and again, the vital green sprang from her fingertips, rising through the blue.

It was a fuller expression of feeling than she had ever created before and she knew it. She knew it in the same way she knew when Mimi was near. She sensed it.

On and on she painted. She painted without pause. Blue and green, light and life. The colors coming into being through the motions of her hands. Form and color in perfect harmony.

Mimi liked the painting. Sunny could tell. She never turned around to look at Mimi. Not once. But she knew Mimi liked the painting.

And on Sunny painted, inspired, enthralled. The expanse of blue above, peaceful and pure, radiating in every direction. The green below, growing, proliferating, striving upward. Ever upward. And the place where they touched, where the green and blue met, bliss transformed into color.

XIX.

Plump red tomatoes hung on their stems, heavy and ripe and ready to eat. Mimi and Fae gently plucked them and laid them in a shallow woven basket.

Then they gathered spinach leaves and lettuce leaves, carefully removing each leaf without tearing it. They piled the rich green leaves in the basket with the tomatoes.

The bell peppers were next. Each pepper started out green and was now as yellow as the sun. A second basket was needed to hold them all.

The carrots and radishes came last. Mimi showed Fae how to grasp the leaves at the base and pull the root out of the earth. Soon the second basket was as full as the first.

Mimi took one basket and Fae the other. They placed the baskets on their heads and carried them inside. The others were waiting. When they saw Mimi and Fae laden with baskets, they were quick to help. Ryder took Mimi's basket and put it on one of the low tables. Wave did the same with Fae's basket. Sunny and Tripp arranged six floor cushions around the table.

Then the feast began.

The tomatoes were sweet and juicy. So juicy that within a few bites they all had juice running down their chins. They laughed as they wiped their mouths and went back for more.

Next they tried the bell peppers. Wave picked one up and flicked its firm smooth skin with his finger. It made a satisfying hollow sound. He did it again and again, tapping out a rhythm. Everyone else bit into the crisp yellow fruit and savored the sweet flavor.

Each root and leaf and fruit had its own taste. Its own unique scent and texture and color. So everyone had a favorite or two. Fae liked the spiciness of the radishes. Tripp especially enjoyed the leafy taste of the lettuce and spinach. He rolled each leaf into a cylinder before eating it.

Tripp looked abstracted as he ate, as if he were deep in thought. And indeed he was. He was composing a poem. Everyone noticed and no one disturbed him.

His book lay open in his lap. The words of his poem gradually appeared on the blank page. They changed as he thought, combining themselves one way and then another until they were just the way he wanted them. When his poem was ready he looked up from the page.

Everyone stopped crunching carrots to listen.

Hues of the harvest:
Green, yellow, orange, and red—
The beauty of time.

They all clapped and insisted on hearing it recited again. Then the feast continued.

The food was filling. Unlike their usual food, the vegetables were wholesome and substantial and nourishing. And the nourishment would last. The vegetables would sustain them much longer than their usual food. Sunny wouldn't have to interrupt her painting as often to eat. Wave wouldn't have to set aside his instruments as often and Fae wouldn't have to stop dancing as often.

Unlike their usual food, this food was hearty. And as they ate it, they gradually became full.

XX.

Stewardship was an honor bestowed only upon the best of scholars. Stewards created the universal prosperity. They protected everyone from natural disasters. They kept at bay the tigers that roamed the outer region. These feats could only be performed by the most learned men and women. Ryder always aspired to be one of them. He studied rigorously in the hope of earning a turn at stewardship. And all of his studying was rewarded. His opportunity had come.

Mimi was fascinated by Ryder's explanation of stewardship. Tripp and Sunny listened with interest too, even though they already knew what stewardship was. They were just so proud of him.

As they sat on the sofas listening to Ryder, Fae and Wave joined them. Fae remained standing and addressed Ryder ceremoniously.

"While we painted pictures and wrote poems, you studied. While we danced and played together, you read. While we took our turns going to the Fair, you stayed home thinking about numbers. Formulas and molecules and numbers. You devoted yourself to knowledge and now you are a steward and you will use your knowledge for the well-being of all. For this, we celebrate you."

When Fae finished speaking she bowed her head. So did the others. Mimi saw that the gesture was a sign of respect and she bowed her head too.

Then they lifted their heads and clapped loudly for Ryder. He smiled with humble pleasure as they applauded.

The celebration had begun.

Wave sat on the edge of a sofa and adjusted his djembe between his knees. When it was properly positioned he struck the drum, beating a rhythm with his hands. He varied the sound of his instrument, striking now the center, now the rim, using the palm of his hands, then just his fingertips. Bass tones alternating with sharp ones. Boom! Boom! Slap! Boom! He made the djembe talk.

As he increased the tempo, Fae added the sound of maracas to his rhythm. Cha-cha-cha! She shook the maracas. Cha-cha-cha! She danced to the rhythm.

Mimi and Ryder sprang to their feet and joined in the dance. So did Sunny and Tripp.

They danced with vigor. They danced with joy. Their feet answered to the call of Wave's drum. The mood was festive. It was triumphant. And they bounced and swayed and spun.

They danced without rest and Wave's beat never faltered. They never got weary or drowsy or spent. Except Mimi of course. She could never keep up. She always got tired and needed to sleep.

She went to the wall and slid open her door. Her body still moved to the music. She turned around once to look at the others. Fae with her maracas. Wave on the drum. Tripp and Sunny dancing to the beat.

Mimi yawned a deep yawn and the music throbbed on.

Ryder was nowhere in sight.

XXI.

The house was half empty. Tripp and Fae had gone to the Fair and Ryder was with the stewards.

Somewhere in the house Sunny was painting. And Mimi was reading or sleeping or gardening. Wave didn't know. He was focused on his music. It had been his turn to go to the Fair, but he was working on a composition so he gave his turn to Tripp.

It was not the first time Wave had given up his turn to one of the others. When he was creating a new piece of music he didn't want to stop.

Tripp was happy to take an extra turn. He had many poems to bring to the Fair and he derived much pleasure from hearing the poems of others. It was only at the Fair that he got to talk to other poets. And he always brought home the best poems he had heard.

Fae loved going to the Fair too. She loved it so much that she couldn't fathom why anyone would give up a turn. With Ryder she understood a little. Ryder was different. But when Wave or Sunny chose not to go she was astonished. So she chuckled when Wave said he was staying home.

"You're funny," she teased. And he liked the way she said it.

Wave had been making progress with his composition, but then he got stuck on a riff. It didn't sound right. He tried it over and over, this way and that, and it still didn't sound right. He needed to clear his head.

He picked up a lute and plucked a simple melody. The sweet notes were soothing. He allowed his mind to relax, to refresh itself after its labors.

Then he heard it. A loud crash. One moment, there was nothing but the silence and the lute. The next, a crash and a blinding white light. He dropped the lute and jumped to his feet. He couldn't see a thing. But he didn't need to see to know what it was. To know who it was. It was the two intruders who escaped during the first invasion. They were back.

They had waited until the household was most vulnerable. It was a clever strategy. To wait and attack when the numbers were even. When Tripp and Fae and Ryder were away. It was a clever strategy, but a hopeless one. And surely they knew that. Surely they knew they were only bringing about their own deaths. But they couldn't help it. They had to try even though they were doomed to fail. Doomed to die.

Wave understood. It was what anyone would do. It didn't make sense. But it wasn't a matter of sense. It was a matter of need. Having come so close to a Felicity, the yearning would be unbearable. The need to try would be irresistible. It didn't make sense, but it was what anyone in their position would do.

Wave knew his life was in danger. The intruders would die. That was certain. But they would kill him first if they had the chance. They would kill him and Sunny too. Wave knew this, but he couldn't see a thing. He could only stand firm and listen for any sound that would reveal the intruders' movements.

He heard nothing but he suddenly saw something. A flash of black. He felt it too. It brushed against him. It was Mimi.

A club fell to the floor as the man wielding it was devoured. It fell right at Wave's feet. The intruder had been directly in front of him and he had not known. In another second the man would have brought the club down on Wave's skull. Had Mimi not been there, Wave would have been killed.

He was momentarily dazed. He didn't even see the second intruder meet her fate, nor the forlorn look on her face before she perished.

The sound of Sunny's rapid footsteps roused him. She ran up to him. They looked at each other, relieved. Then at Mimi. She was sitting on a sofa, slumped forward. Wave picked her up, cradling her limp body in his arms. He carried her to her room.

Sunny followed. She stood in the doorway as Wave entered with Mimi. He bent down to lay her on the bed.

Sunny viewed the scene with the eye of a painter. It was picturesque. The warm orange bed cover with its red and brown design, the vivid blue of Mimi's kimono, the illumination of the multicolored fairy lights. And in the center of it all, the two figures, two gently curved lines.

Wave carefully lowered Mimi's head onto the pillow. Then he lingered for a moment near the soft still form on the bed. He felt glad to be alive.

XXII.

Mimi sat up slowly. She had not slept well and she woke up feeling slightly disoriented. She remembered the invasion. Not all of it. But enough of it to know it was the cause of her discomfort.

She had felt this way once before. She didn't remember much about that either. It was more like remembering a dream than remembering something that really happened. But she felt fairly certain that it had happened. And now it had happened again.

The scent of jasmine tea distracted her from her thoughts. She picked up her cup and drank it in small sips. Her thoughts turned to her garden.

She set down her empty cup and got out of bed. Then she slid open a door to the courtyard.

Something was wrong. She looked all around. Everything seemed as it always did. The stone tile patio, the rattan furniture, the blue sky. What was wrong? Then she saw it. The garden.

The garden was overgrown. The lettuce and spinach had gone to seed and weeds were choking the plants. Fruit was rotting on the vine. How long had she slept?

Mimi went inside. Tripp was reading poems to Sunny, Fae, and Wave. Mimi walked up to them and looked at them firmly. "The garden is dead," she said. Her voice was clear and strong. "Why didn't you tend it?"

They were momentarily taken aback. They had never heard Mimi speak before.

Fae stood up. "I'm sorry Mimi. I didn't even think of it," she said.

"I didn't think of it either," said Sunny. "I was painting."

"I was writing poems," said Tripp and he glanced at the book in his lap.

Wave looked at the floor. "I'm sorry," he said in a quiet voice.

"Let's plant it now!" Fae exclaimed. Her suggestion was enthusiastically received. They all went to the courtyard. The garden was ready to be sown.

First they sat Mimi on a lounge chair so she could rest. She had only just woken up after the exhausting ordeal of the invasion. It was too soon for her to exert herself. Then they planted the seeds. They worked quickly and cheerfully.

Mimi watched them work. They didn't understand her vexation. She thought it peculiar that they wouldn't keep up the garden for themselves. The food nourished them so well that they didn't need to eat so much.

When Mimi was told to eat as much and as often as she could, she didn't really understand. She didn't understand that she would be spending most of her waking hours eating the ginger snaps that were always in her bowl.

The others had to eat almost as much as she did. For every hour they weren't eating, they would have to eat more later to make up for it. This didn't much affect Tripp, who could eat while he read and wrote poetry, or Ryder, who could eat while he studied. But it was especially difficult for Fae. She couldn't eat while dancing. Sunny too. She couldn't eat while painting. Though at least she could contemplate her work while she took time out to eat. Wave could listen to whatever composition he was working on while he ate. But for Fae, eating simply meant not dancing. And Fae would dance nonstop if she could.

If they had tended the garden, they could have reduced the amount of time they spent eating. They could have had more time to devote to their arts. But it just didn't matter to them.

So Mimi thought it peculiar that they didn't keep up the garden. But she didn't think about it for long.

When the sowing was complete, they all went inside. They sat on the sofas and ate their usual food from their bowls.

Fae, Sunny, and Tripp talked. Wave was oddly silent.

XXIII.

A ring of blue light hung in the air. Mimi had never seen anything like it.

Fae created more rings of blue with the small white rod she held in her hand. "I saw it at the Fair," she said. "Would you like to try?"

Mimi nodded eagerly. Fae handed her the rod.

It appeared to be nothing more than a stick of wood, but when Mimi waved it in the air it left a line of blue light that lasted for a few seconds before fading. Mimi was delighted. Fae handed her a second rod. One that made lines of purple light.

Then Fae whirled two rods skillfully, leaving trails of red and orange light. Mimi imitated her movements. Soon the space between them was filled with abstract shapes and arabesque designs. Some were magnificent and some were mundane. But they all shone just as brightly and they all faded just as quickly.

Fae and Mimi frolicked in the shifting colors and patterns. They danced through the afterimages of their own creations.

Music played. "Dark Star." Mimi heard it. Fae seemed to hear it too. They danced to the music.

Then Wave was with them. He was moving to the music. "Is this your music?" he asked Mimi. She nodded. "I like it," he said. He gave a slight nod of his head. Mimi smiled with pleasure at the compliment.

She didn't know where her music came from. It was just there. And until now she was never even sure anyone else heard it.

Fae handed Wave two rods and he joined their dance, adding green and yellow light to the ever-changing patterns. And the music played.

XXIV.

Everyone noticed the change. Mimi had been spending more time among them and less time alone in her room. So Tripp was not really surprised when he saw her sitting on a sofa reading.

One time the others had come to him to ask about the change in Mimi. They asked if there was anything in the lore that might explain it, but Tripp knew little lore. Ryder might know. When he returned from stewardship they would ask him. But until then, it would remain a mystery. A happy mystery.

Mimi looked at Tripp and smiled when he sat down. He asked her what she was reading and she showed him the book. *Life is a Dream*. He read the title out loud, pondered it a moment, and pronounced it a profound poem.

Mimi opened the book to the first page and handed it to Tripp. He read silently. When he reached the bottom of the page he hesitated. Then he lifted the page and took a tentative peek at the other side. There was more text, so he turned the page and resumed reading.

As he was reading, Fae and Wave arrived. They waited until Tripp looked up from the book to speak.

Sunny was creating a mural and they were all going to view it together.

The mural began right where Tripp and Mimi were seated. It was less abstract than anything Sunny had ever painted. There were figures. The figures were abstract. Mere shapes. But they were still figures.

Tripp returned the book to Mimi. She laid it on a table. It didn't matter where she left it. No matter where she left it, it was always nearby when she wanted it.

They all stood before Sunny's painting. The flowing lines of the painting suggested movement. They all stood before it and admired the lines and colors and sense of motion. Then they followed the curve of the wall.

Mimi glanced backward. Her book was not on the table. She didn't expect it to be.

The painted figures were repeated at regular intervals. Each time in different poses and different combinations. Each time suggesting different motions and evoking different emotions. Each scene was unique.

They walked on. Occasionally they paused to consider a scene or discuss some element of the mural. As they walked, Mimi's music played, and they danced as they walked. They bounced along to the music and they listened to the poetry that was part of the music.

Mimi liked walking with them. She liked being with them and listening to them talk. It was pleasant. It felt good.

They walked for what seemed like a long time. Sometimes they ate as they walked. But no matter how long they walked they never caught up with Sunny. How far ahead was she?

Mimi wondered whether they would ever come to the end. Whether they would ever come full circle. She wondered if the wall and the mural painted upon it might go on and on without an end. But that couldn't be. Surely they would catch up to Sunny eventually. Though she knew she would probably tire before that happened. Still she wondered.

XXV.

Ryder was home. And he was more content than he had ever been. His turn at stewardship had been a success. He had fulfilled his aspiration and performed well. Now he was at peace.

He still spent most of his time on his studies, for he hoped to have a second turn, but he joined in the amusements of the others more than ever before. He danced and played without feeling like he should have been studying.

Sunny tossed the little fabric ball to him and he smiled a blissful smile when he caught it. A moment later he tossed it to Wave.

The five of them laughed as they played. It was good to be home.

Mimi was asleep in her room. Ryder observed the same change in her that the others had noticed. She was only in her room when she was sleeping. When she was awake, she was among them.

Ryder explained to them that she was aging. She was more than halfway through her life. Her age was probably the reason for the increase in sociability. The older she got, the less she liked to be alone.

They listened to Ryder with interest. Never before had they been curious about lore, but now they were. Because it was about Mimi.

Ryder reminded them that the lifespan of a Felicity was only about one-third the length of their lives. They knew, but it was easy to forget. She looked the same as she did the day they captured her. They all did.

"She seems more like a sixth than a Felicity," said Fae.

Everyone agreed. Everyone except Ryder. He knew what Fae meant and he shared the sentiment. But in fact, Mimi wasn't a sixth. She was a Felicity. Ryder understood this. And he accepted it.

He enjoyed the time he spent with the others. He took pleasure in their painting and poetry, their music and dance. But what he liked more than anything was when Mimi sat beside him reading as he studied. Just the two of them, sitting together, side-by-side. No sound but the periodic flick of paper as she turned the pages of her book.

He tried it once. It didn't appeal to him. But he liked the sound of it. It was the sound of Mimi sitting beside him.

XXVI.

Sometimes a household had only five. Like Ryder's household. It didn't happen often. But it happened. And when it did, it was lamentable. It was something that could not be controlled. Something unpredictable. Like tigers.

Ryder's household had been five from the beginning. They never even knew the sixth. She died when she was born.

A household of five was forever incomplete. This affected Ryder more than the others, but he didn't give it much thought. It was what it was. Thinking about it would not change it. He concentrated on his studies.

He was still young. They all were. But soon they would pair-bond. Soon they would mate. They were almost a third of the way into their life cycle, the age when mating occurred.

Forming the pair-bond was always a simple matter. The development of their love was gradual and natural. There were no jealousies. No rivalries. No broken hearts. When they mated, they mated for life.

Each pair reproduced only once. Gestation was long but it was easy and there was no discomfort during birth.

The mother always bore twins. A boy and a girl. These offspring matured quickly. They were full grown in less time than they spent in the womb. Once they were adults, they looked the way they would for the rest of their lives. They would get older, but they would never look older.

Juveniles were independent-minded, a trait that was encouraged. The mother and father taught them everything they needed to know and when they were ready they went to their own households. And both mother and father let them go. They reared them well and then they let them go freely. With love, but without attachment.

Parenthood was a brief episode in their long lifespans. Once the offspring were on their own, the mother and father still had two-thirds of their lives ahead of them. And they lived the rest of their lives just as they had before. Unchanged in their interests and pursuits. Eventually they died of old age. Painlessly. Without fear or regrets. Life was good.

Ryder was still young. They all were. And soon they would pair-bond. Soon they would mate. He already felt the urge. He felt it with Mimi. But Mimi was a Felicity.

Soon Sunny and Tripp would mate. Everyone could tell. They were so happy together. And between Wave and Fae the love was growing like a vine reaching toward the sun.

If the sixth had not died in infancy, Ryder would have had a mate. He too would have sired offspring. But if he had that life, he would not have this one. This life that he cherished.

XXVII.

Fae and Mimi danced with scarves. Long iridescent scarves made of colors that morphed as they moved. Colors that streamed across the sheer fabric as they danced. Danced to Mimi's music.

Everyone liked Mimi's music.

It wasn't long before Mimi felt weak, so she stopped dancing and sat on a sofa. The scarf was limp around her neck and shoulders. Its colors flowed to the rhythm of her breath.

Fae looked baffled. Why did Mimi stop so soon? Ryder read her look. He was sitting on the sofa across from Mimi. He looked up from his book. "Mimi's old," he reminded her. "She tires quickly." Fae knew it was true. But she wished it wasn't.

She sat beside Mimi. A book lay in Mimi's lap. Fae had never been interested in books. She liked the poems Tripp read aloud from his book. They sounded nice. And they didn't last long enough for her to get restless. But books didn't really interest her. Not until now. Now she was interested in Mimi's book. She was interested because it was something Mimi liked.

Mimi handed her the book. At first she just delighted in the feel of the book in her hands. Its cover was smooth and supple. Then she read aloud the words printed on the cover. Four words in gold letters. *The Gospel of John*. She didn't understand them, but that didn't trouble her.

She opened the book and read. She pronounced each word carefully. Her voice was sweet and clear. When she finished the first paragraph she lifted her head. She had no need to read further.

A look of ecstasy graced her face and her eyes shone. She sat speechless. Awed by the ineffable something she had but glimpsed. The infinite wisdom that lay in those mysterious words. And the promise of joy, boundless and pure. She smiled at Mimi in gratitude.

From faraway came the faint sound of bongo drums. Wave was playing. Fae heard it first. Then Mimi. Then Ryder. The volume increased and Fae stood up. She moved to the beat. The drumming intensified. Instead of her scarf she held a tambourine in her hand. She gave it a jingle and danced away. The music faded as she went.

Ryder looked up from his studies. It was silent. He met Mimi's eyes and they smiled at each other. A comfortable familiar smile. They looked each other deep in the eyes as they smiled and their look said more than a hundred words. More than a thousand words. Their look said it all.

XXVIII.

Mimi was dying. She could tell. It didn't hurt. It just felt like everything was fading away. Becoming more and more distant. Unreal.

Ryder knew she was dying. He told the others.

She had been lying on a sofa for a long time. She slept there. She ate there. And all the activities of the household happened there, where Mimi was lying. So she wouldn't miss anything that happened.

But now she was dying. They brought her into her room and laid her on her bed. The cold, Ryder hoped, might prolong the time she had left.

The five of them sat on cushions by the side of her bed. She could see them all. The room seemed bigger than before. Perhaps it was bigger. They all fit comfortably. They shouldn't have. But they did.

Ryder, who sat nearest her, wore a thick beige sweater over his kurta. So did Wave and Tripp. Fae and Sunny had wrapped themselves in heavy white shawls with long woolen fringes.

Mimi drifted in and out of sleep. Whenever she awoke, she wondered whether she had slept for a long time or just a few moments. But it didn't matter. All that mattered was that each time she opened her eyes they were all there.

Sunny and Tripp were holding hands. Holding hands tightly. As if they could protect each other from the loss that was coming. They were beautiful. They were all beautiful. Mimi looked at each of their faces as they kept vigil around her deathbed.

Ryder moved closer. He sat on the edge of her bed and caressed her cheek. She almost spoke. She even opened her mouth to speak. But she didn't.

She had only spoken two times in her life. Both times because she needed to speak. But she didn't need to speak now. She had nothing to say. She had lived a good life and now it was over. Nothing she could say could mean more than this moment. This moment she was living with them. This moment they were living with her.

Ryder took her hand in his.

The multicolored lights cast rainbows on the paper door screens. Music came from somewhere. "Brokedown Palace." She could barely hear it. But it was there.

She never found out what she was. Or why they brought her here. But it didn't matter. She was happy. They gave her a happy life. And she loved them.

Mimi smiled. She gave Ryder's hand a squeeze. Then she died.

XXIX.

Silence. They bowed their heads. Mimi was dead. It was the time of mourning.

Sunny and Tripp were the first to stand. Sunny went to the wall and started to paint. She painted a figure. The figure was Mimi. Surrounding her were five other figures. Like the spokes of a wheel. The sky was red.

Tripp watched her paint. Then he opened his book and began to create a poem.

> *The hunt, the capture*
> *In the rosy glow of dawn—*
> *Felicity found.*
>
> *Mimi, our Mimi—*
> *Unfathomable and wild,*
> *Rarest of creatures.*
>
> *A boon to our home,*
> *Fresh blossoms borne on a breeze—*
> *The fragrance of spring.*

Fae arranged Mimi's hair, fanning it prettily over the pillow. Then she straightened her kimono. She smoothed the left sleeve but not the right. Ryder was still holding Mimi's hand.

Sunny moved across the wall painting scene after scene.

She painted a lone figure in blue reclining on a bed of dark orange.

Then she painted figures dancing in a circle. One figure held a guitar. The other five seemed to leap lightly in the air. Bright colors swirled around them.

Next she painted a whirlwind of black. Five figures huddled behind the whirlwind. Other figures seemed to be fleeing.

Simple and asleep—
Waking to color and sound,
Poetry and dance.

At home in our home—
Peaceful in her cool dark den
And playful with us.

Golden sun at noon
Searing the green summer grass—
Radiant, deadly.

Wave still sat beside Mimi's bed.

Sunny painted a garden. A figure tended the garden.

She was something new—
Philosopher, gardener,
An artist of life.

Lonesome ways outgrown,
This solitary being—
She grew in wisdom.

Autumnal sunset,
Deepening orange, crimson—
The beautiful world.

Sunny painted two figures sitting side by side. They each held books.

She aged in silence—
Invisibly declining,
But rich in spirit.

Short-lived enigma,
Much more than lore predicted—
She was one of us.

Moonless winter night—
Mimi is dead. Cloudy sky,
Cold white barren snow.

Wave stood up and brought his harmonica to his lips. He cupped his hands around it and made it wail and moan. He played the blues for Mimi.

Sunny painted a funeral in gray. Five figures in a circle. Heads bowed. In the center, a figure lay. A lone spot of blue in the circle of gray.

Mimi's book lay on the low table beside her bed. Fae picked it up. She brushed her fingers over the gilt lettering of its cover. Then she opened it in the middle. The left page was blank, but three lines were printed on the right page. She read them to herself.

In the beginning was the Word,
and the Word was with God,
and the Word was God.

Fae smiled. She held Mimi's book to her chest. It seemed that Mimi had finally found a poem she really liked. One she wanted to read over and over. The only one she wanted. Perhaps she finally understood.

Wave stopped playing. His song was done. He put his arm around Fae.

Then Sunny painted her final scene. There were two figures. Next to the two figures stood two smaller figures. One of the small figures pointed to the blue sky. The other held a book.

When Sunny bears young,
We shall name them Sky and Lore—
In Mimi's honor.

Tripp's poem was complete.

Ryder pressed Mimi's body to his breast. He held her tightly and buried his face in her hair.

XXX.

The funeral was finished. They celebrated Mimi's life the only way they knew how, and now the funeral was finished. They stood solemnly at her bedside. All except Fae.

Fae slid open a door to the courtyard and stepped out into the twilight. She picked wisteria flowers and piled them into a basket. Then she came back inside.

The heady perfume of the wisteria filled the tiny room.

She laid each flower on Mimi's bed. Sunny helped. Tripp, Wave, and Ryder stood against the white walls to give them space to move. Soon Mimi's body was surrounded by the bluish-purple blossoms.

The light was dim. They took one last look. It was a beautiful sight. Beautiful and melancholy.

Then they left the room and the door closed for the last time. Closed as if it had never been.